Do Pirates Take Baths?

Kathy Tucker
Illustrated by Nadine Bernard Westcott

ALBERT WHITMAN & COMPANY
MORTON GROVE, ILLINOIS

Also by Kathy Tucker
Do Cowboys Ride Bikes?

Text copyright © 1994 by Kathleen Tucker Brooks.
Illustrations copyright © 1994 by Nadine Bernard Westcott.
Published in 1994 by Albert Whitman & Company,
6340 Oakton Street, Morton Grove, Illinois 60053.
Published simultaneously in Canada by General Publishing, Limited, Toronto.

Printed in the United States of America.
10 9 8 7 6 5 4

Library of Congress Cataloging-in-Publication Data
Tucker, Kathy.
Do pirates take baths?/written by Kathy Tucker ; illustrated by Nadine Bernard Westcott.
p. cm.

Summary: Humorous rhyming answers to thirteen questions about the life of pirates.
ISBN 0-8075-1696-1 (hardcover) ISBN 0-8075-1697-X (paperback)
[1. Pirates—Fiction. 2. Stories in rhyme.] I. Westcott, Nadine Bernard, ill. II. Title.
PZ8.3.T793Do 1994 94-4109   [E]—dc20
CIP   AC

For Jerry, my favorite pirate. K.T.

For Becky. N.B.W.

WHAT DO PIRATES DO?

All day and night,
they sail the seas;
they're very brave and bold.
They count the gulls
and watch the waves
and search for chests of gold.

HOW DO YOU GET TO BE A PIRATE?

You show the captain,
who picks the crew,
that you're a special case—
that you can run
and kick and climb
and make a fearsome face.

WHAT DOES A PIRATE WEAR?

A big black hat,
some swell black boots,
an eyepatch to make you stare;
he carries a cutlass,
but I've been told
he doesn't wear underwear!

WHAT DO PIRATES EAT?

Salty cod
(or sometimes scrod)
with hardtack that's tough to chew;
they never eat pizza—
instead, they dine
on seaweed and barnacle stew.

HARDTACK

DO PIRATES WORK HARD?

At breakfast time,
they swab the deck
and pull the rigging tight.
They dance the hornpipe
after lunch,
then have a jolly fight.

DO PIRATES TAKE BATHS?

Just once in a while,
when they smell *very* bad,
they jump into the seas.
They use sea foam
to wash their hair,
and shells to scrub their knees.

DO PIRATES HAVE PETS?

They keep a parrot;
Polly's her name.
She knows how to talk to a mate:
"Shiver me timbers!"
"Walk the plank!"
"Pass me some pieces of eight!"

WHY DON'T PIRATES GET LOST?

They know that the sun
comes up in the East
and sinks into the West.
They know that the *X*
on their secret map
marks the treasure chest!

Sand Bar

Island with Banana Trees and Monkeys

Buried Treasure

Land Where Their Mothers Live

Pod of Whales

Dangerous Rocks

Stormy Weather

N
W ⭐ E
S

HOW DO PIRATES CAPTURE A SHIP?

They sneak up slow . . .
then storm the deck,
beating a big red drum!
Flashing their swords,
they give a shout,
"Surrender, cowardly scum!"

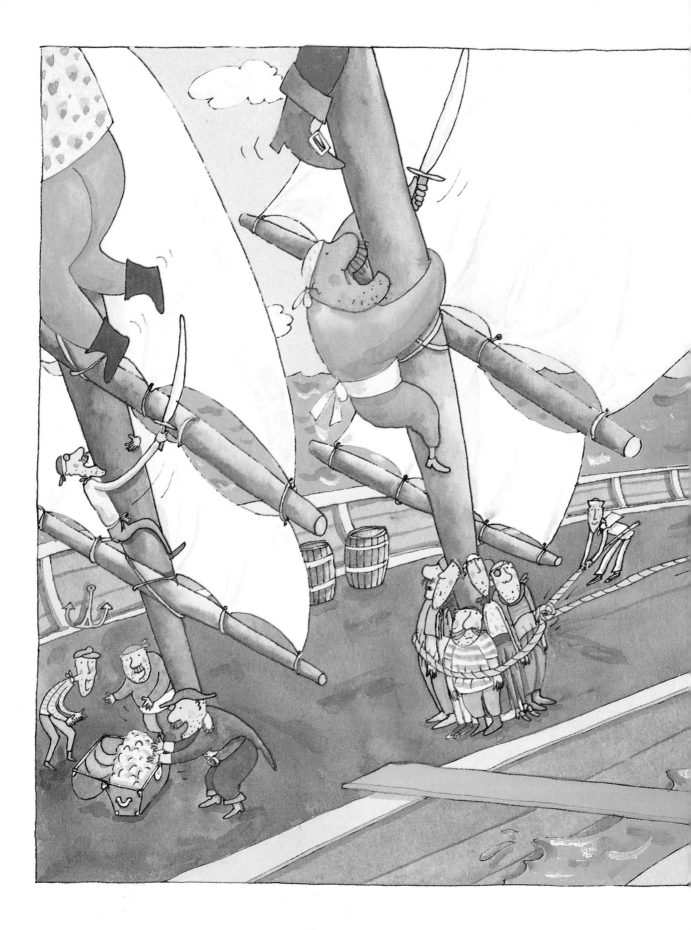

They fight their way
to the top of the mast
(they hardly ever fall),
then tie up the captives
with good strong rope,
and blast a cannonball.

HOW DO PIRATES DIVIDE THE GOLD?

"One piece for you,
two pieces for me—"
"Hey, you're not being fair!"
Ten for the captain
'cause he owns the ship
and doesn't want to share.

DO PIRATES HAVE BIRTHDAYS?

Of course they do—
with presents and games
and lots of soda pop.
The cook makes a cake
with doubloons inside
and a skull-and-bones on top.

WHAT DO PIRATES WISH FOR?

They wish for an island
with gold in the sand,
where the sun shines over the bay—
where banana trees grow,
and pirates are free
to swing with monkeys all day.

WHERE DO PIRATES SLEEP?

On cozy hammocks
way down in the hold,
they sway till the morning light.
They dream of their mothers
as they gently drift
into the starry night.